AuthorHouse™
1663 Liberty Drive
Bloomington, IN 47403
www.authorhouse.com
Phone: 1 (800) 839-8640

Because of the dynamic nature of the Internet, any web addresses or links contained in this book may have changed
since publication and may no longer be valid. The views expressed in this work are solely those of the author and do
not necessarily reflect the views of the publisher, and the publisher hereby disclaims any responsibility for them.

Any people depicted in stock imagery provided by Getty Images are models,
and such images are being used for illustrative purposes only.
Certain stock imagery © Getty Images.

This book is printed on acid-free paper.

ISBN: 978-1-7283-5884-0 (sc)
978-1-7283-5885-7 (e)

Print information available on the last page.

Published by AuthorHouse 04/14/2020

authorHOUSE®

The Lady and the Dog Take a Train

Eugene Ugrumov
Artist credit: Eugene Ugrumov

The Lady and the Dog

Once there was an occasion

At Pennsylvania Station.

A lady had checked in her baggage:

A chest, a chair, a large package,

A basket, a hatbox, and an antique clock.

And last, but not least, her very small dog.

The lady was given a receipt for her baggage:

For the chest, the chair, the large package,

For the basket, the hatbox, and the antique clock.

And last, but not least, for her very small dog.

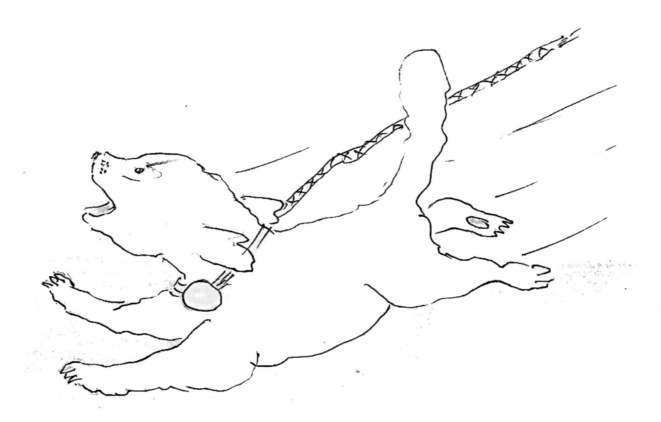

But just before the train

Set off on its way,

From the train's baggage car,

The dog ran away.

The train was nearing its destination.

It was now arriving at Union Station.

The baggage conductors discovered in fear—

The dog disappeared! Oh, the dog disappeared!

They counted again every piece of the baggage:

The chest, the chair, the large package,

The basket, the hatbox, and the antique clock.

Every item was there except for the dog!

Suddenly, right next to the carriage,

Appeared a shaggy and very large dog.

They grabbed it and added him to the lady's baggage:

To the chest, the chair, the large package,

To the basket, the hatbox, and the antique clock—

Instead of the lady's runaway dog.

With a handcart a porter was pushing the baggage:

The chest, the chair, the large package,

The basket, the hatbox, and the antique clock.

Behind him his helper was pulling the dog.

As the dog loudly growled

The lady cried out—

"This dog is another breed,

This is not what I need!

Is this some kind of joke?

Give me back my cute little dog!!!"

"Excuse me, dear madam, but everything
is according to your receipt.

This morning you checked in your baggage:

The chest, the chair, the large package,

The basket, the hatbox, and the antique clock.

And, of course, your lovely very small dog.

However, it's clear your dog has grown a jiff,

During the train's long trip"

WHAT DOES A MOUSE FEAR?

Tell me, please, right now and quickly—

What does a mouse fear?

A mouse fears a crafty cat,

And nothing, nothing else.

What does a cat fear?

It fears only a dog!

A fierce, huge, and shaggy dog,

And nothing, nothing else.

What does a dog fear?

A dog fears its master!

It fears only its master,

And nothing, nothing else.

The dog's master is courageous!

What can frighten him now?

He fears his stern wife,

And nothing, nothing else.

A woman doesn't fear anything!

Of course, she doesn't feel fear!

She's brave and isn't afraid of

Anything in the world.

Indeed, doesn't she feel afraid?

She fears a little mouse,

Only a little mouse,

And nothing, nothing else!

What does a mouse fear?

Printed in the United States
By Bookmasters